Jimmy's Leprechaun Trap

Surely leprechauns are cute little fellows who do no harm to anyone? **Be warned!** They are nasty little creatures, just waiting for the chance to trick someone and gain power over them.

When Jimmy meets up with one of them, very strange things start to happen. But how can he get rid of him? Does Grandfather have the answer? Can they trap this clever little fellow and outwit him?

Jimmy's Leprechaun Trap was shortlisted for the Bisto Book of the Year Award 1998

Dan Kissane

Dan Kissane was born in London and lived at first above a pet shop. At the age of two, he moved to Bedfordshire, taking his parents and two brothers with him. There, he taught himself to read, write, play the tin whistle and ride a bicycle. After leaving school, he headed for County Kerry and now lives on a small farm where he keeps sheep and bees. He still plays the tin whistle and occasionally rides a bicycle. His ambition is to do both at the same time!

Dan's other books for children

Jimmy and the Banshee
Pugnax and the Princess
The Eagle Tree

JIMMY'S LEPRECHAUN TRAP

DAN KISSANE

Illustrated by Angela Clarke

THE O'BRIEN PRESS
DUBLIN

First published 1997 by The O'Brien Press Ltd.,
20 Victoria Road, Rathgar, Dublin 6, Ireland.
Tel: +353 1 4923333; Fax: +353 1 4922777
E-mail: books@obrien.ie; Website: www.obrien.ie
Reprinted 1998, 1999, 2001.
ISBN: 0-86278-512-X

British Library Cataloguing-in-Publication Data
Kissane, Dan
Jimmy's leprechaun trap
1. Children's stories
I. Title II. Clarke, Angela
823.9'14 [J]

4 5 6 7 8 9 10
01 02 03 04 05 06

The O'Brien Press receives
assistance from

Typesetting, layout, editing: The O'Brien Press Ltd.
Cover illustrations: Angela Clarke
Cover separations: C&A Print Services Ltd.
Printing: Cox & Wyman Ltd.

Words you may need to know:
Tír na nÓg –
the Land of Youth, where the fairies live
(pron. Teer nuh nogue)

the Little People –
the fairies

clochán –
a mound of stones often seen in a field and said
to belong to the fairies *(pron. cluckawn)*

pegged –
threw (in Kerry speech 'he pegged it'
means 'he threw it')

CONTENTS

1 Lambing *page* 7

2 The Creature 11

3 Leprechaun! 17

4 The Secret 21

5 Grandfather's Yarns 26

6 Two Funny Things 31

7 The Third Funny Thing 42

8 The Weird Egg 50

9 The Trap 56

10 A Wakeful Night 59

11 The Treasure 65

12 Missing! 69

13 Riddles 73

14 The Challenge 81

15 The Test 86

16 Nearly Tricked! 91

17 The Wayward Hen 94

For Allison

LAMBING

As I remember, it was in the month of April that it all started.

April is a busy time on a sheep farm, because it is then that the young lambs are born. That particular April, the weather was very fine and sunny and I was feeling rather important because my father had kept me at home from school to help look after the sheep. I didn't mind missing a few days' school, though I would have liked Mikey McGrory, or one of my other friends, to keep me company. But, like I said, it was a busy season and I didn't have time to be lonely. My job was to sit in the field during the day and keep an eye on the ewes in case any of them got into difficulty while lambing. If that happened, I was to go for help.

Have you ever seen a lamb coming into the world? It's quite amazing and rather wonderful, really, but at the time of which I am writing, I had seen so many being born that I didn't really take a lot of notice of them. What happens is that one moment the ewe is walking about and the next moment she starts to act funny. She stops eating and goes away to the side of the field on her own. Then she starts sniffing the ground and scratching it with one of her front legs. After a bit, she lies down, and eventually, after a lot of straining and groaning, the lamb comes out and shakes its head. It's very wet and slimy first of all, but its mother soon licks it clean and dry.

That's what usually happens, but sometimes the lamb bends its legs awkwardly so that it can't come out. It's something like when you're putting on a pullover and you get your head stuck in the arm. You have to get someone to sort out your arms and help you get your head out. That's what I had to watch out for.

On this particular day, I had been on watch since just after breakfast-time and nothing out of the ordinary had happened. Two lambs had been born without any trouble and I was finding it pretty hard to pass the day. By the time the sun was high in the sky, I was beginning to feel hungry and was looking forward to my dinner. The ewes were all grazing happily and I decided it would be safe to leave them unattended for the half-hour or so it would take for me to run home and get a bite to eat.

Before I left the field, I took a last quick glance to make sure they were all okay, and it was then that something caught my eye. In the middle of the field there was a big heap of stones, or as we say in Irish, a *clochán*, and as my eye swept across it, I saw something move: something small and slender, like a bird, but not a bird. When I saw it, it was looking at me, but as soon as it realised that I had seen it, it disappeared under the *clochán*.

I stood where I was for a minute, scratching

my head. I couldn't quite believe what I had seen. Then I began to wonder if I *had* actually seen it. I walked across to the *clochán* and looked at the spot where I thought it had been. There was a small hole there, like a rabbit burrow, only not so big. I got down on my hands and knees and peeped into it, but I couldn't see anything. Could I have imagined it? I asked myself. I got up and headed for the gate; but as I went, I had a strong feeling that something was staring at my back, and I didn't think it was a sheep.

2

THE CREATURE

I walked home slowly, thinking over what I had seen. Along the laneway which I followed, little green shoots were just beginning to sprout out on the brambles, and I picked a few and chewed them as I walked.

When I got home, my father was in the yard, splitting logs with the hatchet for the fire.

'Are the sheep all right, Jimmy?' he asked as I walked past him.

'They are,' I answered.

'Don't be long now with your dinner and get back to them.'

I went into the house. On the table there was a steaming plate of floury boiled potatoes, their skins broken as if they were smiling at the prospect of being eaten. My mother was straining cabbage out of a saucepan, and in the corner by the fire my grandfather was puffing away at his pipe.

'Here's the young shepherd!' he cried as I came in. 'Sit up to the fire and tell me all the news.'

'Never mind the news,' said my mother, placing a plate of hot bacon and cabbage on the table, 'here's your dinner.'

Grandfather knocked the dottle out of his pipe and we sat down together. My father came in, hung his cap on the back of the door and took his place at the head of the table. After we had said Grace there was no talking for a while because our mouths were busy, but after a bit my father said:

'Anything out of the ordinary this morning, Jimmy?'

I shook my head but kept quiet: I wasn't sure whether I ought to say anything about what I'd seen.

My father had stopped his fork half-way to

his mouth. 'Well?' he said at last. 'Has the cat got your tongue?'

'I ... I ... I saw something in the field.'

'Something?' repeated my father. 'What was it?' Suddenly a gleam came into his eye. 'Was it a fox? I'll get my gun ...'

'Don't tell him, Jimmy,' said my grandfather. 'The fox must live too!'

Grandfather always said that, and when he did my father would go mad. He hated foxes: he suspected them of killing young lambs during the night. A big argument started now between the two of them. I think it would have gone on forever if I hadn't interrupted them.

'It wasn't a fox,' I piped up when they paused for breath.

They both looked at me. 'What was it then?' they asked together.

I didn't know what to say. In the end I got up from the table and fetched a piece of paper. 'I'll draw it,' I said. I wasn't much of an artist, I'm afraid, but I did my best. This is what I drew:

When I had finished I handed it to my father. He held it at arm's length and stared at it.

'What's so strange about a grasshopper?' he asked at last, throwing the paper on the table where my grandfather picked it up.

'That isn't a grasshopper!' he said. 'That's a squirrel!'

My mother came around behind his chair and stared at my drawing. 'It's neither one nor the other,' she declared. 'That's a frog standing on its back legs!'

Then the three of them started arguing, trying to grab my drawing and shouting: 'Grasshopper!'

and Squirrel!' and 'Frog!'

Grandfather's false teeth fell out of his mouth and landed in the butter, but he didn't take any notice. He just kept on shouting 'Squirrel!' except now it came out: 'Shquirrel!'

Of course, my drawing wasn't meant to be any of those things, but once my family started arguing there was no stopping them, so I just got up and tiptoed out and left them at it.

3

LEPRECHAUN!

As I walked back to the lambing field I was feeling sort of mixed up. Before dinner I had been quite sure of what I'd seen, but now I was beginning to have my doubts: such things just didn't exist. Maybe it *was* a squirrel, or a grasshopper, or even a frog standing on its back legs! But just then, all these thoughts were driven out of my head. On my way to the field I had to pass our cabbage garden and what was inside but John Sullivan's red cow, chomping away at our cabbages as though cabbages were creations of the devil and she had been appointed by God to rid the world of them.

I hopped over the ditch and grabbed up a handful of stones. I pegged a couple at her, but in a half-hearted sort of way, because I had always been fond of that cow and I didn't want to hurt her. Anyway, she got the message and with a skittish shake of her horny head she took a flying leap over the ditch and landed outside in the road. A bit further along I found the place where she had broken out of Sullivan's field and when I had coaxed her in, I fixed up the fence.

After all that, I was anxious to get back to the sheep, so I hurried on. Two ewes had lambed while I was away and the little lambs were nuzzling under their mothers' bellies, looking for their first important drink of milk. The ewes stared innocently at me, as if to say: '*We* couldn't help it; *we* wanted to wait till you came back, but *they* insisted: *you* know what *lambs* are!'

There was an old whitethorn tree in the corner of the field, its branches gnarled and twisted with age. Grandfather had told me that it looked that way even when he was a young boy, so it must have been very old indeed. It was flushed now with the wonderful green of the new leaves, and I sat down under its shade. Its blossoms were not yet open, but the little white flower buds were there, ready to burst as soon as May arrived. Here and there around me, young ferns were pushing their bent heads up through the ground, and all along by the ditch dandelions were holding up their golden faces to be kissed by the droning bumblebees that blundered from one to the other. By and by, I heard a cuckoo shouting in the distance, telling the country around of his return from the sunny shores of Africa, and what with all the peaceful sights and sounds, and the dinner which had settled itself nicely in my stomach, I fell sound asleep.

*   *   *

It was a fly walking on my nose that woke me. I shook my head and looked around: the sun was still high in the sky, so I knew I had not been asleep long. But straightaway I had to rub my eyes, and rub them hard! And then I knew for a fact that what I had seen earlier hadn't been a grasshopper or a squirrel – or a frog standing on its back legs either! For there he was! Standing at my feet! There was no other way to describe him: he was a Leprechaun!

4

THE SECRET

'How many did you tell?' he demanded, with his little chin sticking out. And even though he was so small, I was very frightened of him. There was just something so ... mischievous – yes, that's the word – *mischievous* about him. *Mischievous* and *pointy*! You know how some people have pointy noses, or pointy chins? Well, *everything* about *this* person was pointy! His nose, chin and ears; his elbows and his knees; his hat – even the ends of his shoes! His clothes were all different shades of green, and if he stood completely still, he became almost invisible.

But he didn't stand still for long. He hopped from one foot to the other and demanded again, in his pointy little voice: 'Answer me!

How many did you tell?'

'Beg pardon?' I said, in a sort of half-whisper. 'How many *who*? And what am I supposed to have *told*?'

'I know you saw me earlier!' he said accusingly. 'And I know what children are! You ran off straight away and told your parents! And maybe the police! And maybe even the newspapers! And before we know it,' he continued, getting ever more agitated, 'half the country will be here searching for my gold!'

'But I didn't!' I protested, sitting up straight. 'At least, not the police, and not the newspapers! And as for my parents, they didn't understand.'

That seemed to calm him down a bit and he stood still. It was amazing the way he seemed to disappear. I could just make out his outline but to all intents and purposes he had vanished. If I hadn't known he was there I wouldn't have given him a second glance.

'Oh?' he said after a moment. 'So you mean

to say you're the only one who knows about me?'

I nodded. 'And as for your gold – ' I said, but he gave a little jump and interrupted me:

'Gold? Who said anything about gold? Did I say *gold*? What I meant to say was er ... *OLD*! Yes! That's it! Old er ... old socks! Yes! I meant to say they'd be here searching for my old socks! *Gold*! What an idea! Where would I get gold? That's all a myth about Leprechauns having pots of gold! *Gold*! *Indeed*! ' And he gave a little laugh which I thought sounded forced.

Neither of us said anything then for a little while. He stood looking at me and I sat looking at him, or what I could see of him, because he was standing still again. Then it got sort of embarrassing. It always seems to be that way when you meet someone and you can't think of anything to say, and *they* don't have anything to say either: it doesn't seem the right thing to just sit there and stare. So after a bit I said: 'The weather is good, don't you think?' or, at least, I began to say it, but I only got as far as 'The weather ...' because he blocked me by asking: 'How old is your grandfather?'

I thought that was a strange question because I couldn't fathom how he knew I *had* a grandfather. But I didn't want to be impolite, so I said: 'He's old: he was alive at the time of Noah's Ark, and that was ages ago.' Grandfather had told me all about Noah and how he had helped him build the Ark, so I knew he had been there. Grandfather didn't tell lies, although sometimes I suspected him of being a little careless with the truth. The Leprechaun gave a little shudder, and I thought for a moment that he might have been laughing.

'Oh,' he said, 'he *was*, was he?'

'Yes,' I said, anxious to impress him with Grandfather's great age and knowledge, 'and he knows all about Adam and Eve too, and Fionn McCool, and all those other people from long ago.'

'I see, I see,' said the little man, nodding.

'Well now, listen here to me: I know that boys and girls find it hard to keep a secret, so if you want to, you can tell *him* about me, but it's very important that you don't tell anyone else. Now, I have to go, because I have work to do, but if you're here tomorrow, I'll give you a story to tell.' And with that, without waiting for any reply, he gave a little jump and pointed at something above my head. I looked up to see what was there, but there wasn't anything, and when I looked back he was gone!

(5)

GRANDFATHER'S YARNS

We had fish for supper that evening – mackerel, I think it was, or it might have been herrings, I can't quite seem to remember – but I know I ate them fast. I wanted to get finished so I could do my evening jobs and get around to talking to Grandfather. I had to give hay to the cow, and feed the pig, and then I had to make sure that all the hens were gone in to roost and see that the henhouse was securely closed for fear the fox would come in the night.

Everything was going fine until I got to the hens. I counted them over and over, but there was one missing, and it didn't take me long to realise that it was the same old hen as usual. She was always the first one to arrive at feeding time but she was always missing when it came time to close up the henhouse. I hunted around for her for ages, but I couldn't find her, and in the end I got mad and wished bad luck on her and hoped that the fox *would* get her. Then, just as I was about to close the henhouse door and let her take her chances outside for the night, she appeared out of a clump of nettles, saying 'Bock-bock-bock!' to herself and making it plain that, whatever about me, she was in no particular hurry. You'd swear she was a Golden Pheasant instead of a scrawny old hen.

Anyway, it wasn't long after that I was sitting in front of the fire with a mug of tea, listening to Grandfather. He was telling me a story which I won't go into now because it would take too long, but when he came to a stop, and began refilling his pipe, I said:

'Grandfather, do you know anything about Leprechauns?'

'Leprechauns?' he said, cocking a bushy eyebrow at me. 'I should *think* I do! Why, wasn't there a Leprechaun used to live in that very field where you've been all day! When I was a young lad I saw him often! Bohannon, his name was – The Little Bohannon. Many's the time I spoke to him, and a right little terror he was! I had a dog called Pagan, and one day when we were in the field, Pagan ran after him and tried to catch him. D'you know what happened? The Little Bohannon put a curse on him! All of a sudden Pagan started chasing his own tail, and when he caught it, he started eating himself! First his tail, then his legs, then his body! In the end, all that was left was his teeth! I'm telling you, that taught me a thing or two about Leprechauns!

'But that's a long, long time ago,' the old man finished. 'There are no more Leprechauns in Ireland now. Like the wolf and the eagle and the giant deer, they're a thing of the past.'

I wanted to jump up and say: But they're not! I've seen one!, but my mother was sitting at the table, sewing, and I remembered what the little man had said about not telling anyone except Grandfather, so I bit my tongue and kept it in.

But I had to know more. 'Where did they go?' I asked.

'The Leprechauns?' said Grandfather. 'Why, they went away back to Tír na nÓg. At least that's what The Little Bohannon said the last time I saw him: "We're away out of this place, my friend," he told me. "Off home to Tír na nÓg. Nobody believes in us any more, and when you're an old man we'll be just a memory: the stuff of legends."'

Grandfather paused here, took a pull out of his pipe and spat into the fire. 'And d'you see, Jimmy? He was right! Here I am,' he concluded, 'an old man; and the Leprechaun is just a legend.'

He was going to say more, but my mother butted in. 'I do wish,' she said, 'that you'd stop filling the boy's head with that old nonsense! Leprechauns and Tír na nÓg! He's too old for that simplicity! And as for you, young man,' she added as she tidied away her sewing things, 'it's time you were in bed.'

I got up from my chair and said goodnight, but before I left the kitchen I managed to whisper to Grandfather: 'He's *back*. I saw him today!'

Grandfather didn't say anything. He stared at me for a second, and then, turning his face back towards the fire, he spat into the flickering flames.

6

Two Funny Things

It seemed that I had been asleep for only about five minutes when I felt someone shaking me and pulling the bedclothes off. I sat up and rubbed my eyes. It was just getting bright, and I could see my father looking down at me.

'It's six o'clock, Jimmy, time you were up.'

I pulled myself out of the bed and struggled into my clothes. I found it very hard to make my eyes stay open, but my mother had left out a cup of milk for me and some bread, and after I'd eaten, I didn't feel so sleepy. I stuck on my boots and headed off out. The air was chilly, but it looked as though it would be fine later on. Everything seemed just as usual: John Sullivan's red cow was lying down in her field, chewing her cud, and she stared at me as I went past, just as usual – but I thought for a second that she winked at me, almost as if she were party to some secret.

It was when I got to our own field that I came across the First Funny Thing. All the sheep had broken out and were scattered around the road and mountainside. If the gate was open I could have understood, because sometimes a sheep would scratch herself against it and shake the catch loose. But it wasn't – it was shut. I opened it and tried to chase the sheep back in, but it was no good; they would go as far as the gate, but no farther. There was only one thing to do, and I did it: I went home for Spider.

Spider was our sheepdog, and a right good sheepdog he was – I had trained him myself. Admittedly, he didn't always do the right thing, but rounding up the sheep was usually no problem for him. I hurried back to the yard and untied him; we always kept him tied up over-night because it's very important not to let dogs

loose in sheep country. And the next minute we were away over the road again, Spider dancing out before me, delighted with his freedom, sniffing into rabbit burrows and enjoying himself generally, the way dogs always do.

The second he saw the sheep, he stiffened. He crouched down, stared at them, and looked up at me with a sort of hunted expression. I could almost hear him asking: What will I do?

'Keep outside 'em, Spider!' I said, making a sort of circling motion with my arm. 'Bring 'em on!'

Spider shot off like a black-and-white torpedo, and before you could say 'Scissors!' the sheep were all gathered up in a bunch, so close together that you couldn't get the leg of a spoon down between any two of them.

'Steady now, Spider,' I said softly. 'Nice and easy.'

Slowly and carefully, Spider walked along behind the flock, all the time steering them towards the open gate. But it was no good:

nothing in the world would make them go back into the field. I shouted and waved my arms, and Spider shouted – in his own way, of course – and waved his tail, but all to no effect. It was as if there was an invisible barrier across the gap and they just couldn't go through.

I stopped and scratched my head. 'There's only one thing to do now,' I said to myself. 'I must take them home and put them in the field behind the house. But I don't know what Dad is going to say.'

Without more ado, I fell into place behind the flock and, with Spider's help, got them moving along the road towards home. Then I remembered I had left the gate open so I ran back to close it. I glanced into the field as I did so, and what did I see but the little man on the top of the *clochán*, dancing a jig and killing himself laughing.

'I suppose you think that's funny!' I shouted at him.

He stopped laughing, but kept right on with

his little dance. 'It's my field, laddo!' he cried. 'And I'll decide what's going to be in it. That's the story I promised you! Tell it to your father!' And with that, he jumped down and disappeared into his hole. There was nothing more I could do, so I set off after the sheep.

By the time I had got them installed in the field behind the house, it was nearly nine o'clock, so I went in for a cup of tea.

My father was sitting at the table, knocking the top off a boiled egg, and he looked up at me in surprise. 'What are you doing home?' he asked. 'Is anything the matter?'

I told him what had happened, though I didn't say anything about the Leprechaun, because I didn't think he'd believe me. He gave a little laugh and went back to his breakfast. 'That saves me a journey,' he said. 'I was going to walk over and shift them anyway. There isn't much grass left in that field and they're getting hungry. I expect that's why they broke out.'

Of course, I knew better, but I said nothing.

I sat up to the table and my mother put an egg in the saucepan for me. My father glanced up at the clock. 'I must get a move on,' he murmured. 'John Sullivan is coming with his tractor and trailer at nine o'clock. We're going to clear away the *clochán*.'

My mouth fell open, but before I could say anything, my grandfather appeared in the kitchen doorway, yawning and scratching his chin. 'What's that you said?' he asked.

'That old heap of stones in the lambing field,' my father explained. 'It's about time we cleared it away. Then we can plough the field and set turnips.'

Grandfather's face registered horror. 'Clear away the *clochán*?' he repeated. 'Set *turnips*? *You can't be serious*! That *clochán* has been there for hundreds of years. It'll bring bad luck.'

'Why? It's only an old heap of stones.'

Grandfather began to object again, but my father cut him short. 'I'm not going to argue about it,' said he. 'I must get cracking. John

Sullivan will be there before me.' And with that, he wolfed down his breakfast, shoved back his chair, and stood up. 'Keep an eye to the sheep, Jimmy,' he added, making the sign of the cross. And he took his cap from the back of the door, settled it on his head and went out.

Grandfather sat down wearily at the table and stared at me. 'Something bad will come of this, Jimmy,' he said, closing one eye and screwing up his mouth. 'The Little People are not to be interfered with!'

* * *

Everyone knows what happened next. At least everyone around *here* heard about it. My father and John Sullivan went at the *clochán*, but they had only shifted two or three stones when the Second Funny Thing happened. The tractor was standing alongside them, with the engine switched off, when all of a sudden it started up by itself and took off across the field – without any driver!

My father and John Sullivan went racing after it, shouting 'Whoa! Whoa!' the same as if it were a horse, but of course it took no notice. They thought it might stop when it came to the fence, but no! It just crashed straight through, rolled on down the hill and finished up by throwing itself into the river!

That was bad enough, but the two men were running so hard behind it that when they came to the riverbank they couldn't stop, and before they knew it, they were up to their ears in the river too.

My father was very forlorn-looking when he came home. He was soaked to the skin, his trousers and boots were all mud, he had lost his cap, and there were bits of twigs and waterweed stuck in his hair. He was in a terrible temper, and he got even madder when Grandfather said: 'I knew it would happen. Haven't I told you a hundred times not to interfere with the Little People?'

Father took a deep breath and I think he was

about to tell us what he thought of the Little People when my mother interrupted him and made him go away and change his wet clothes.

Grandfather looked at me and winked. When he got me on my own, he said: 'This is only the beginning, Jimmy. The Little Bohannon won't stop at that. They should never have tried to interfere with his property. It's unknown what he'll do next!'

'Isn't there anything we can do?' I asked. 'Can't we stop him?'

Grandfather stuck his pipe in his mouth and lit it. 'There is only one way to put a stop to the mischievousness of a Leprechaun,' he said, puffing out a cloud of fragrant smoke, 'and that is by catching him. And one of the hardest things in the world to catch is a Leprechaun! But,' he added, with a twinkle in his eye, 'we can try, Jimmy!'

7

THE THIRD FUNNY THING

The next day, my father had to stay in bed because he had caught a cold by falling in the river. My mother sent me out to feed the hens and told me to bring in whatever eggs had been laid. The earth around the henhouse was bare where the hens had scraped away the grass, and just as I let out the squawky inmates, I thought I noticed some pointy little footprints around the door; but by the time the hens had all run out, there was nothing to be seen except *their* footprints, so I couldn't be sure.

In the henhouse, there were several little boxes laid on their sides, each with a nest of straw inside. Usually, when you put your hand into one of these in the morning, you would find two or three smooth warm eggs, just waiting to be collected; but this morning was different: it was the Third Funny Thing. All the nest-boxes were empty! Not an egg to be found!

I went in and told my mother. She put her hands on her hips and stared at me. 'What do you mean "no eggs"?' she demanded. 'There must be eggs there! Them hens are the finest hens I ever had! And they're laying away by the new time! I got sixteen eggs yesterday – I sold them to Mrs Dunphy. Go and look again!'

I shrugged my shoulders. 'There's no point; there's no egg there – not as much as one!'

Grandfather arrived in the kitchen just then, and my mother didn't waste any time before telling him about the eggs. He didn't say anything; he just looked at me. We both knew it was more of The Little Bohannon's mischief.

When my mother wasn't looking, Grandfather beckoned to me with his head and I followed him out into the yard.

'Didn't I tell you he was only starting?' he said.

I nodded. 'Well,' he continued, 'it's time we got started too. We have a Leprechaun to catch!'

After breakfast, I strolled back into the field where the sheep were. In this field there was a great boulder, which made a handy seat for me. I sat down and looked around. The sheep all seemed fine, but I seemed to see Leprechauns peeping at me from all over the place. My head was so full of them now that I half-expected the sheep to start having Leprechauns instead of lambs. I hadn't been there very long when Grandfather joined me.

'Now, Jimmy,' he said, easing himself down beside me on the rock, 'the first thing you have to do before you try to catch something – and it doesn't matter whether it's an elephant or a Leprechaun you're after – is to make sure that you know everything there is to be known about your *quarry*.'

I had always thought that a quarry was a place where they broke up stones, but he explained to me that it was also a word meaning something you were trying to catch.

'The quarry in this case being a Leprechaun,' he went on, 'I will now teach you all I know about them, which is nearly everything, and what I don't know isn't worth knowing.'

I had to get up at that point to rise up a sheep that had got thrown on her back. They do that sometimes when they're itchy: they lie down and wriggle around to scratch the itch and then find that they can't get up again because all their legs are in the air. If they lie that way for too long they will die, but once you roll them over, they jump up and off they go. I did it, and when I got back to the boulder, Grandfather had settled himself more comfortably and had lit his pipe.

'Leprechauns,' he began, gazing away into the distance, 'are a race of beings found only in the island of Ireland. Their real home is Tír na nÓg, the Land of Youth, which lies somewhere away in the ocean, far to the west. But when they come amongst mortals, they live only in Ireland. They are small in size, usually not more than twelve inches in height, and often even less than that. Long ago, they were very plentiful. You would often meet them in fields, on mountainsides, by rivers, in woods, and sitting on the tops of stone walls, but nowadays they are very seldom seen, and only when they themselves choose.

'They live for a very long time – hundreds of years – and their chief delight is in making mischief. They love to open gates so that cattle and sheep can stray – as we have seen. They can cause hens to stop laying – as we have also seen; and nothing gives them more pleasure than turning milk sour, making dogs bark at night and causing wasps to sting for no reason.'

'But why do they do all that?' I asked.

'Ah!' said Grandfather, blowing a smoke ring into the air, 'that's a good question. Unfortunately there isn't a good answer. I suppose they do it for the same reason that anybody gets up to mischief. But the great thing about Leprechauns is: if you leave them alone, and don't interfere with them, they won't interfere with *you*. But once you draw them on you ... well, then it's *you* or *them*! '

'But what do they do when they're not making mischief?' I enquired. 'Don't they have to make a living or something?'

'Well, by trade they are shoemakers, and it used to be said that if you could get a pair of shoes made by one of them, they would last forever – not like the shoes you get now, which you can almost wear out coming home from the shop where you bought them! But, like many tradesmen, they have no great liking for their work. They are always looking for an excuse to go off and get up to mischief. And the slightest excuse will do: just look at John Sullivan and your father – they only shifted a couple of stones from The Little Bohannon's *clochán* and that was enough!'

'But maybe,' I suggested, 'if we just left him

alone now, he'd be satisfied and wouldn't bother with us any more ...'

Grandfather gave a short laugh. 'The Lord save us! But the innocence of youth is a wonder to behold! Haven't you been listening to anything I've been saying, Jimmy? That Leprechaun won't rest now from making mischief till he's worn himself out, and by then your father and the rest of us won't be worth a hatful of crabs. So it's up to us to put a halt to his gallop!'

I was going to object again, but I could see by the way the old man was puffing his pipe that his mind was made up. The fact is, the more I heard about this Leprechaun, the more afraid of him I was getting. It seemed to me that someone who could stop hens from laying and make a tractor throw itself into the river, and all those other things, was going to be a bit too much for an old man and a young lad like myself.

'What'll we do, so?' I said, a little reluctantly.

'What I said. We'll have to catch him, and the

best way to do that is with a trap – a Leprechaun Trap!'

'What's that?' I asked.

Grandfather took the pipe out of his mouth
and prodded me gently in the chest with the
stem. 'You leave that part of the job to me,
Jimmy,' he said firmly. 'I'll attend to that.'

8

THE WEIRD EGG

When we went into the house at dinner-time, we found that my father had got up. He was sitting by the fire with a blanket around his shoulders and a scarf tied around his neck. Every now and then he would give a great loud sneeze or get a fierce fit of coughing. In between sneezes and coughs, he looked up and addressed my mother: 'Is that egg boiled yet?'

I looked across at the cooker and saw a little saucepan bubbling away happily. 'Where did you get the egg?' I asked in wonder.

'Oh!' said my mother in a kind of accusing tone, 'you may say that you searched the hen-house well this morning–'

'What do you mean?' I said.

'I'll tell you what I mean,' said she. 'I went

out to check and found a fine big brown egg in the first box I looked in. And here it is!' she added, taking it out of the saucepan with a spoon, like a conjuror pulling a rabbit out of a hat. She set it into the egg-stand that was waiting ready on the table.

My father gave a gigantic sneeze, stood up and pulled his chair across to the table. I noticed that Grandfather was staring at him with a kind of frown on his face. My father picked up the egg in one hand and a spoon in the other, and as he did so, Grandfather said quietly, 'I wouldn't eat that, if I was you.'

My father glared at the old man. 'Oh, you wouldn't would you? Well, maybe if you were as hungry as I am, you'd eat it!'

'I wouldn't,' Grandfather persisted. 'That's not a proper egg.'

'What do you mean?' put in my mother. 'It couldn't be any *more* proper! Sure I tell you, I only got it out of the nest a couple of hours ago!'

My father sneezed, shook his head wearily and said: 'Proper or not, I'm going to eat it!' And with that, he drove his spoon through the shell and cut the top off the egg.

OH! The SMELL! I will never forget it for the rest of my life! I had never smelled anything like it before, and never want to ever again! It was so bad that I can't even begin to describe it properly to you, but if you want to get an idea of the smell that came out of that egg, here is what to do.

Take an old sock that someone has been wearing for about two weeks. Into it put a bit of dead fish, some rotten chicken guts, a few bad potatoes, a piece of mouldy cheese and half a pound of dog's droppings. Boil all that for an hour in a saucepan of horse's sweat, and you will have a vague idea.

(It is best to ask your mother's permission before trying this experiment.)

Anyway, when the smell burst upon us, we all reacted in different ways. My mother ran to

the dresser where there was a big vase of wild spring flowers and she stuck her face in amongst them. My grandfather stuck his pipe in his mouth, lit it up as fast as he could and started puffing away furiously. I hopped across to the window and stuck my head out. My poor father came off the worst because he was holding the egg, and the cloud of vapour that came out sort of wrapped itself around his head. He jumped to his feet and shouted something that sounded like: 'Baughhh!'

Then he did an unfortunate thing: he pegged the egg. I don't think he knew where he was pegging it – he just wanted to get rid of it. But the fact is, it struck my mother on the back of her head and got all mixed up in her hair. She pulled her head out of the vase of flowers and let out a screech that nearly stopped the clock.

My father dropped his blanket and ran out through the door. I still had my head out the window, so I was able to see all that happened next. My father was crawling around on his

hands and knees outside, gasping and coughing and saying 'Baughhh!' and 'I'm finished!'
But the most amazing thing was my mother. I
had never realised that she was so athletic. She
came tearing out the door after my father and
passed him out with a flying leap. We had a
big trough of water in the yard that the cow
drank out of, and what did my mother do but
run across and stick her head into it!

In the midst of all this, I heard my grandfather talking to me. 'Pull in your head, Jimmy,'
he said, 'the smell is mostly gone out.'

I did what he said. He was standing by the
table, wreathed in clouds of tobacco smoke.
He didn't say any more. He just looked at me.
And I looked back. We didn't need to say it: it
was more of The Little Bohannon's mischief.

9

THE TRAP

The Leprechaun trap was the most wonderful contraption I had ever seen. It looked like a cross between an old bicycle and a beer-crate, which is not surprising because they were the things Grandfather used to make it. There was a sort of pedal thing in the front which was rigged in such a way that, if a Leprechaun stood on it, it would jump up and send him flying head-first into the beer-crate. A little gate made of bicycle spokes would close over the crate – and hey-presto! the Leprechaun was caught!

The only thing I couldn't see was how we were going to get the Leprechaun to stand on the pedal. I said so to Grandfather.

'Bait, Jimmy!' he replied. 'Same as fishing.

The right bait will catch anything.'

'But what's the bait for Leprechauns, Grandfather?'

Grandfather frowned and scratched his head. 'That's the only bother. The right bait is *gold*. They just can't resist it.'

'Gold?' I cried. 'But where would *we* get gold, Grandfather? Isn't there anything else?'

'Well ...' he said doubtfully, 'I suppose we could try bread-and-milk. They're supposed to be fond of that, too ...'

We carried the trap out and put it next to the henhouse that evening, because we knew The Little Bohannon had been that way before and we thought it likely he might come snooping around there again. When it was set up to our satisfaction, we placed a little saucer of bread-and-milk inside. Grandfather had brought some sugar, wrapped in a twist of paper, and he sprinkled that on top. 'If that doesn't draw him, I don't know what to say,' he said, standing back and looking at the trap with a satisfied air. 'Now come along in.'

'But how will we know if he goes into it?'

'Aha!' said Grandfather proudly, 'that's the ingenious part. D'you see that string?' he asked, pointing to a length of thin cotton which was tied to the pedal of the trap.

I nodded.

'That string goes all the way to the house and in through my bedroom window. When I get into bed, I'll tie the end of it to my big toe. The big toe on my left foot is very sensitive and if The Little Bohannon steps on the pedal, it will pull the string and my toe will feel it. And anything my toe feels,' he added, 'I feel too!'

I was amazed. I had never realised before just how clever my grandfather was.

'Now, you be ready during the night,' he warned me as we went in to our supper. 'If my toe feels that string pulled, I'll need your help, and quick!'

(10)

A WAKEFUL NIGHT

I ate my supper very quickly that evening and
hurried off to bed. I wanted to get some sleep
in case I had to get up during the night. But it
wasn't any good. I just couldn't seem to drop
off. After a bit I got up and tiptoed across to the
window and peeped out. The moon was up
and I could see the trap clearly, over next to
the henhouse, but there was nothing in it and
everything was quiet, so I went back to bed.
I tried even harder then to get to sleep. I
twisted this way and that way; I screwed my
eyes up tight; I put my head under the
blankets; I even tried counting sheep, as if I
hadn't had enough of that during the day!
But it was no use: nothing worked. I decided
to give up and stay awake all night. And no

sooner had I decided that than I fell asleep!

The next thing I was aware of was the sound of a dog barking. I opened my eyes and straightaway I knew it was Spider. I would have known his bark anywhere. I thought that there might be a fox around the henhouse, so I jumped out of bed and ran to the window. But it was no fox that was making Spider bark: it was the Leprechaun trap! It was hopping up and down as if it were alive, and rolling over, and shaking itself like a mad thing. I expected every second that it would fly into a hundred pieces.

As quick as I could I ran to Grandfather's room. There he was, lying on his back in the bed with his mouth open, snoring. His feet were sticking out from under the blankets, and as for his sensitive toe – it was in danger of being pulled out of its socket by the string, and he hadn't felt a thing! I shook him hard.

'Wh-wh-wha'sh the marrer?' he spluttered. He hadn't got his teeth in, so it was hard for him to talk properly.

'Grandfather, we've caught him!' I hissed excitedly. 'Look at your toe!'

He sat up straight in the bed and stared at his feet. 'Heart of the Devil!' he cried, grabbing his teeth off the bedside table and sticking them in his mouth. 'I tied the string to the wrong toe. That's my *right* toe: there's no feeling at all in that!' He looked up at me. 'Are you sure it's him? It might be a rat ...'

I shook my head. 'It's no rat. The trap is jumping around like a March hare. It must be him.'

'Right! Get dressed as quick as you can and meet me outside. And don't make a sound.'

I hurried back to my room and jumped into my clothes. I was so excited that, at first, I put my trousers on back to front and my jumper inside out, but I sorted myself out eventually. Two seconds later I was standing outside the house. As soon as Spider saw me, he stopped barking and stood there staring at the trap with his head on one side and his ears standing up.

When Grandfather came out, we walked cautiously towards the trap. It had stopped jumping about now and lay still. 'Be careful all the same,' said Grandfather, 'a trapped Leprechaun is no joke.'

The trap was lying on its side, so we couldn't see into it. Cautiously, Grandfather turned it upright and we peered in. The moon was still bright enough to see by, but we couldn't see anything inside the trap: it seemed to be empty. 'He's gone!' said Grandfather.

I was about to agree when I thought of something. 'Maybe he's just keeping still,' I said. 'When he does that, he's nearly invisible!'

'Oh, he is, is he?' said Grandfather. And picking up a little stick, he poked it in through the spokes. Straightaway we heard a yell and The Little Bohannon suddenly appeared before our eyes, rubbing his stomach. He was grinding his teeth together angrily, and even in the moonlight you could see that his face was very flushed.

'How dare you?' he cried. 'What do you mean by poking me in the belly? Let me out at once!'

'We will,' I said, 'provided that you agree to leave us alone and stop making mischief.'

Immediately, the little man answered. 'All right,' he said, 'I agree. Now let me out.'

Grandfather pulled me aside. 'Life would be very simple, Jimmy,' said he, 'if you could believe everything you hear. But you can't, and this fellow is not to be trusted. Here's what we'll do: I'll stay here and keep him occupied while you run along to his *clochán* and see if you can find anything there. I've a notion,' he added, giving me a wink, 'that there may be a little store of something yellow and shiny ...'

11

THE TREASURE

Usually I was in no hurry when I travelled the road which led to the field where the *clochán* was, but on this occasion my feet hardly touched the ground. By the time I reached the field I was out of breath and my heart was beating like a trip-hammer. I hopped over the gate, skipped across to the *clochán*, and flung myself down next to the hole. One half of me wasn't too crazy about the idea of putting my hand down the hole, because you never know what's in a hole, but the other half wanted to see if there *was* anything down there, so I took a deep breath and reached in. But there was nothing. At least, there was nothing that I could feel, but that was mainly because I couldn't get my hand to the bottom of the hole. I rolled over on my side and reached in even further until all my arm and half my shoulder was inside, but it was no good: either the hole was too deep or my arm was too short. Either way it amounted to the same thing. I pulled my hand out and sat up and had a think.

It was just beginning to get bright, and in the morning light, my eye fell on a length of old rusty barbed wire that was coiled around the gatepost. That was just what I wanted, and in a flash I had unwound it and was lying down by the hole again. Carefully, I shoved in the wire and when it wouldn't go in any further, I began to twist it. At first it went around easily, but gradually it got stiffer, until I couldn't twist it any more. Obviously it was tangled in something, so I began to pull. What could it be? Bit by bit I drew it up towards the top of the hole, and then, suddenly, out it popped into the open. It was a bag – a small leather bag, tied at the mouth with a little leather thong. I sat up straight and untangled it from the barbed wire, and then, with shaky fingers, I opened it.

I expect you can guess what was inside it. Yes, you're right, it was gold! Little grains of gold, each one no bigger than a hayseed! In fact, that's just what they looked like: tiny golden hayseeds! And the little bag was full of them! There must have been thousands!

Quickly I tied up the bag again and, using the two loose ends of the thong, I fastened it onto my belt. Then I was out over the gate in a flash and on my way home. I couldn't wait to show off my treasure!

But there was a surprise in store for me. When I landed into the yard I could see no sign of Grandfather. What I *did* see was the Leprechaun trap, and it was thrown on its side with the little door of spokes hanging open. The Little Bohannon was gone, and he had taken Grandfather with him!

I stood where I was for what must have been about ten minutes, my mouth open in disbelief, just staring at the empty trap. And then I felt something brush against my ankle. My hair stood on end and I began to tremble. I was sure it was the Leprechaun, but I was too scared to look.

But after a bit, when nothing seemed to be happening to me, I plucked up courage and glanced down. And what do you think was there? Nothing more nor less that my old scrawny red hen! She had been missing the night before, when I closed up the henhouse, and I hadn't waited for her. Now she was pecking at something on the ground that looked like seeds. I stooped down to look more closely, and they *were* seeds: little golden seeds. I clapped my hand to the leather bag at my waist, but the minute I touched it I knew I was too late: it was empty! The barbed wire had made a small hole in it and all the little golden seeds had dropped out. My scrawny old red hen had eaten The Bohannon's gold!

(12)

MISSING!

You never heard such a commotion as when my father and mother found out what had happened. My father started shouting that it was all his fault, and that if he hadn't interfered with the *clochán* it would never have happened; and my mother started crying, saying how she would never see Grandfather again. And outside in the yard, Spider heard all the wailing and started howling like a wolf, and then the cock hopped up on the window-sill and started crowing as if he were trying to drown all the others out. It was pandemonium.

I knew this was getting us nowhere, so I slipped out the door and went off to sit with the sheep. I often find that when you're faced with a problem which you can't solve, the best thing to do is to just go away somewhere quiet and forget about it; then the answer often comes by itself. And, believe it or not, that is more or less what happened in this case. There I was, sitting quietly, watching the sheep, when I got this horrible feeling that someone was watching me. I looked to the right and to the left, but I couldn't see anyone. So then I spun around quickly, and, just as I thought, there he was! The Little Bohannon! Right behind my back! He was sitting on a stone, and the reason I could see him was because he was swaying ever so slightly from side to side. I jumped to my feet and started to back away from him, but when he made no attempt to follow me, I stopped and stood my ground.

'Where is it?' he said.

Of course I knew what he meant – his gold. But I didn't think it would be quite the right thing to tell him that my old hen had eaten it, so I answered instead: 'Where is my grandfather?'

He didn't make any reply to that, he just stared at me. And then he began to laugh a horrible thin little laugh. It wasn't the sort of laugh that sounds funny either, but more the sort that someone makes when he's going to do something nasty.

'So!' he said at last. 'We want to play riddles, do we?'

I didn't really know what he meant, but I had to say something, so I said, 'All right.'

He looked at me searchingly. 'I suppose you think you're pretty smart,' he said. And when I didn't answer, he went on: 'Here's what we'll do. I'll ask you a riddle, and if you can answer it, you get your grandfather back. But if you can't, you return my gold. Then you ask me a riddle, and if I can't answer it, I'll go back to Tír na nÓg and never bother you again. But if I *do* answer it ...' he stopped talking and his face broke into the most evil smile you can imagine.

'Yes?' I prompted. 'If you *do* answer it ...'

'If I do,' he said, rubbing his hands together

gleefully, 'you'll be my slave forever!'

The hair stood up on the back of my neck at that, and I'm sure I must have turned pale.

'Do you agree?' he said, and before I had time to think, I heard my voice saying: 'Yes.'

What else could I do?

13

RIDDLES

'Right so,' said the Leprechaun jauntily, 'we'll get started. Here is my riddle:

'Shakes without hands; whistles without lips; cries without tears. Who is he?'

When I heard that, I started to tremble all over. I hadn't an idea of the answer. But I summoned up my last little bit of courage and said: 'You'll have to give me time to think.'

The Little Bohannon clapped his hands and did a little dance. He knew very well I hadn't a clue. 'Oh, I'm not in any hurry,' he said glee-fully. 'I'll give you plenty time: let's say ... this time tomorrow? Meet me here and bring the answer ... *or the gold.* And to show how fair I am,' he added with a snigger, 'I'll bring the old man with me – just in case you *do* answer it!'

And with that, he hopped across the ditch and disappeared.

I sat down and scratched my head. I had never been in a real pickle until now! It was bad enough that the Leprechaun had got my grandfather; now it looked as though he were going to get me too!

I sat there for hours. I decided in the end that there was no point in telling my father and mother – there was nothing they could do anyway and they would only make a fuss. The sheep were all grazing away happily and none of them looked any way likely to lamb, so I went off home. As I came into the yard, Spider jumped about at the end of his chain, barking and wagging his tail in greeting.

That put me thinking. 'Shakes without hands,' the Leprechaun had said, and here was Spider, who had no hands, and he was shaking his tail! I thought of the rest of the riddle: 'cries without tears; whistles without lips.' Well, I reasoned, Spider did have a habit of howling now and again, and that was almost the same as crying, and there were no tears either! So far so good! Maybe I could get Grandfather back after all!

But no matter how hard I tried I couldn't get the third bit to fit. Not by any stretch of the imagination could I see Spider whistling, lips or no lips. The nearest he could get to it was barking when somebody else whistled, and that wasn't the same thing. But I thought I was on the right track, so I went in, ate my supper, and went off to bed.

That night was one of the worst that ever blew. The wind came howling from the east, driving before it sleety rain which it flung against my little window-pane like gravel. I lay awake for a long time, listening to the storm and thinking about the riddle, but eventually I dropped off to sleep. All night long, my mind was filled with dreams of Spider standing on his back legs, whistling a tune called 'The Mason's Apron' and shaking his tail in time to the music.

By morning, the rain had stopped, but the wind was still roaring across the top of the chimney. I had no proper answer for the Leprechaun's riddle, and it was with a heavy heart that I trudged up to the field behind the house. It looked as though I would never see Grandfather again, and it would be all the worse for me when The Little Bohannon found out about his gold!

I went to the place where I had seen him the day before and waited. It was hard for me to stay standing, the wind was buffeting me about so much, but I didn't have long to wait. Soon I heard his voice behind me, saying in a mocking tone: 'Well, riddler, have you got the answer? Or the gold?'

At least I think that's what he said, but he was standing in a gap between two bushes and some of the words got snatched away by the wind.

I racked my brains, but it was no good. I just couldn't think. 'Can't you give me some more time?' I pleaded.

'What?' he shouted, cupping his hand to his ear. Obviously he couldn't hear me any better than I could him.

'More time!' I shouted again.

He seemed to catch on this time, but he shook his head. 'No more time! Answer now!'

I was beginning to get flustered. It seemed hopeless.

'Is it Spider?' I asked in desperation.

'What?' he cried. 'I can't hear you. Speak up!'

'I can't help it!' I shouted. 'It's the wind!'

'What?'

'The wind!' I cried at the top of my voice, pointing up in the air as though the wind was something you could point at and see. 'It's the wind!'

Suddenly the little man's eyes seemed to almost pop out of their sockets. His face grew pale and he began to jump up and down in a rage. Shaking his pointy little fists at me, he cried: 'Someone told you! Who was it?'

He was shouting so loud now that I had no

difficulty in hearing him, but I couldn't for the life of me make out what he was on about. It was almost as if I had answered his riddle. And then it dawned on me. Without meaning to, I *had* answered it! It was *the wind*! Why hadn't I thought of it before? Even now it was shaking the branches over my head. *Shaking without hands*! And it was whistling through the gap where The Little Bohannon was still hopping up and down, cursing! *Whistling without lips*! And it was crying in the trees! *Crying without tears*! I had got it by accident!

But, accident or not, I was entitled to my prize. 'Hand over my grandfather!' I demanded.

He stopped his carrying-on then, and stared sullenly at me. 'He'll be home when you get there!' he shouted. 'And don't forget: now you must ask me a riddle, and if I get the answer right, you're my slave!'

That brought me down to earth again, but I was beginning to feel as if – maybe – it might *just* be possible to get the better of this little mannikin after all!

'Tomorrow!' I said defiantly. 'By the *clochán*, at sunrise.'

He nodded, gave a little jump, and was gone.

The wind was still howling around the field, so I made a quick check of the sheep, and as soon as I was sure that they were all right, I hurried off home. When I arrived, Grandfather was sitting at the table eating a slice of bread and drinking a cup of tea.

14

THE CHALLENGE

I won't go into the rigmarole which took place when my parents found that Grandfather had come back. There was the usual 'thought we'd never see you again!s' and 'where on earth have you been?s' and astonishment and tears and all that, but Grandfather didn't take any notice of it. The fact is, he didn't know where he had been. He remembered that, after I left him, the Leprechaun called him over to the trap and then threw something in his eyes. The next thing he knew he was sitting by the kitchen table and everyone was making a fuss. He had no idea where he had been in the meantime.

After a bit, the excitement died down and I got the chance to talk to him alone. I explained to him what had happened and he listened quietly until I had finished. 'And you mean to tell me,' he said at last, 'that the gold is gone?'

'The gold is gone,' I confirmed, 'and it's only by chance that you're not gone too! And if we can't think up a good riddle for tomorrow,' I added, 'I'll be gone!'

Grandfather pulled out his pipe and lit it. When he had it going well and the blue smoke was curling up to the ceiling, he stood up and said: 'Let's go outside. You can't think properly in a house. You have to have the air flowing around your brain.'

We walked out into the yard and strolled up and down for a bit, neither of us saying a word. Finally we came to a stop by the gate of the meadow, which was the field where we grew our hay each year. Of course, at this time of year, the grass was short and the hens were wandering around in it, scratching for worms.

'So that's the culprit!' said Grandfather, taking the pipe out of his mouth and pointing at the scrawny old red one. 'That's her,' I said. 'She has a king's ransom of gold inside her.'

We stood there for a few minutes, leaning on the gate, and then Grandfather said: 'Come on now, Jimmy, never mind the hens. We have to get thinking about this riddle.'

'How about this?' I said eagerly, suddenly remembering a riddle I had heard at school a few weeks before. 'How much oil would a gumboil boil if a gumboil could boil oil?'

'That's too easy,' sighed Grandfather. 'Everyone knows the answer to that: As much oil as a gumboil could boil would a gumboil boil if a gumboil could boil oil. But what about this one?' he continued: 'Why does it take a blackthorn bush so long to grow?'

'That's an old one too,' I said. 'Because it's a *sloe* bush.'

This went on for about half an hour, each asking the other riddles which we both knew the answers to. At last Grandfather said: 'It's no good, this is getting us nowhere. The best thing is for us to separate and each think by himself.'

And with that, he struck off up the laneway. I watched him go, and he must have been thinking furiously as he went, because he was driving smoke from his pipe the same as if he was an express train. As for me, I went back to have another look at the sheep.

When I got there I saw something I didn't like, but what it was gave me the idea for a pretty good riddle.

*   *   *

For as long as I could remember, Grandfather and I had always been the best of friends. There had never been a cross word between us and we had never come even close to having a falling-out, but that evening we came near to it. It was all because I wouldn't tell him the riddle I had made up. Normally I would have trusted him with my life, but I didn't want to take any chances when it came to my freedom. I was afraid that The Little Bohannon might get to him and I would end up as the Leprechaun's slave. As we sat by the fire after supper, he kept glancing at me from the corner of his eye and muttering under his breath. When I got up to go to bed, he caught me by the elbow. 'If it was me who'd thought it up I'd tell you,' he said in a hurt voice.

I felt sorry for him then, and almost told him, but I hardened my heart at the last second. 'Grandfather, you'll hear it in time enough. I daren't tell you yet; even if I only whispered it *he* might hear. You can't be too careful with Leprechauns.'

'Well, I daresay you're right there,' he agreed grudgingly. 'I only hope it's good enough to outsmart him. Leprechauns are deadly when it comes to riddles.'

'He won't have heard this one before,' I assured him. 'Don't worry.'

I hoped and prayed I was right, but as I got into bed I had butterflies in my stomach. I wondered if it would be my last night sleeping in my own little room.

THE TEST

It's an old saying: 'However long the day, the night always comes.' Well, it works the other way around too: 'However long the night, the day always comes.' Because, although I thought that night would never come to a finish, it did in the end. But there was no more sleep on me than there is on a bee in a field of clover. It was even worse than the night we set the trap for the Leprechaun, and that had been bad enough for anything! I kept on repeating the riddle to myself, changing it first one way and then another and then back again. In the end, I had said it over so many times that I began to think that everybody in the world must know the answer. But I knew I would never be able to think of a tougher riddle, and if The Little Bohannon could answer this one there was no hope for me

After what seemed an eternity, the sun began to edge its way up in the sky and started to shine in through my window. As it did, my heart began to beat faster. I had often heard people saying that when they were worried their heart was in their mouth, and just then I was sure that mine was. I was afraid that if I clenched my teeth they would bite into it and that would be the end of me!

Slowly, slowly I pulled on my clothes and went out of my room. Everybody else in the house was fast asleep, even Grandfather. But I was glad of that: if The Little Bohannon was going to get the better of me, I didn't want anyone around to see it happen. I would just disappear and go off to Tír na nÓg and be a slave and nobody would ever know what had happened to me.

It was the brave side of me that thought that. The other side wanted to run back up the stairs and jump into bed and pull the blankets over my head. But I had learned enough about The Little Bohannon to know that that wouldn't work. He would get me sooner or later, so it was as well to face him now. But I have to admit that there was no spring in my step that morning and my shoes were dragging the ground as I set off to the field of the *clochán*.

He was there before me. When I arrived at the gate, he was standing on top of the *clochán*, hopping impatiently from one foot to the other and muttering to himself. As I walked slowly across the field towards him I began to be able to hear what he was saying. At first I thought he was just reciting nonsense, but then I realised that he was trying out the answers to different riddles!

'Three hundred miles,' he said absently, and then, 'Seven and three quarters', and then, 'Twice daily, but three times on Sundays.' God only knows what the actual riddles were!

He was concentrating so hard that he didn't

see me coming at first, and when he did, he gave a little jump and became quiet. He stared at me with the most horrible expression you can imagine. Then he stooped down and picked up a brass chain which I hadn't noticed lying beside him. There was a heavy brass collar attached to the end of it. 'Know what this is, Riddler?' he said. I shook my head.

'This is a slave-collar,' he said with an evil grin. 'And as soon as I've answered your pathetic riddle – whatever it may be – you'll be wearing it!'

I shivered at that prospect, and my mouth turned dry. I tried to swallow, but the spit got stuck half-way down and made a lump in my throat. He could see how nervous I was and he began to laugh. 'Come now, *Mr Riddler*,' he sneered, 'let's hear your riddle. I bet I can answer it without even thinking!' And he leaned forward, one hand on his hip, the other cupped behind his ear, as if he was anxious not to miss a word.

I began to tremble. All of a sudden, my riddle seemed ridiculously simple. He was bound to know the answer. Oh, why hadn't I thought harder and made up a more difficult one? But now it was too late. In a faltering voice, I said:

'A black diner
At breakfast seen,
At a white table
On a carpet of green.
What was he?'

16

NEARLY TRICKED!

'So what happened next?' Grandfather said. It was later that morning and I was explaining the whole thing to him.

'Well, the first thing was that he stopped his laughing and then he turned pale. And then he sat down on top of the *clochán* and began to cry. He couldn't answer it! "It's not fair!" he sobbed. "I gave you an easy riddle, and you've given me a stinker!" D'you know? I began to feel sorry for him! Guess what he did then. He dried his eyes, gave a little cough and said: "Give me a clue, just a little one. I won't say the answer, really I won't – it's just for future reference." And he nearly fooled me. I was just about to give him a clue when I spotted the gleam in his eye, a wicked, deceitful gleam. He was trying to trick me!

'"No!" I cried. "Answer up now, or get back to Tír na nÓg! That was the bargain!"

'At that, he suddenly gave a loud and terrible yell. He began to jump up and down in a rage and wave his arms about and kick at stones. He snatched his pointy little hat off his pointy little head and began tearing it to pieces and stuffing the pieces into his mouth! I had never seen anyone or anything so angry in all my life! And then there was a dazzling, blinding flash of light, and ... he was gone!'

While I was explaining all this, we had been walking up behind the house towards the field where the sheep were.

'But what about the riddle?' said Grandfather, when I had finished. 'What was the answer?'

We had just arrived at the gate of the field, and I put my finger to my lips. Cautiously, we peeped over the gate. There was the thing I had seen the day before. I hadn't liked it then, and I didn't like it now, but it had saved me.

In the middle of the field, one of the sheep had died. She lay there still, a white lump on the green grass. And sitting on the carcass, pecking away at the flesh, was a black raven.

'A black diner!!' said Grandfather. 'At a white table, on a green carpet!'

17

THE WAYWARD HEN

By the end of the week our little household was back to normal. My father's cold had cleared up and we had nothing more to say about The Little Bohannon. I had been forced to repeat the story of my adventure over and over again until everyone knew it off by heart.

After supper one evening, my mother said, 'Go out now, and close in the hens.'

Out I went and counted the hens who had gone into their little house by themselves. And, as usual, there was one missing. And you can guess which one it was! Yes, the scrawny old red one!

I was about to give up on her, when I heard her bock-bock-bocking in the nettles. Only this time, she didn't seem to be making any move to come home. After a few minutes, I got impatient, and I decided to look for her. I poked around in the nettles, parting them with a stick to avoid getting stung. It didn't take me long to find her, and the reason she hadn't come in was obvious: she had made a nest in the nettles and she was sitting on it.

Very gently, I lifted her off. And when I saw what was under her, my mouth fell open. They were eggs, of course, but no ordinary eggs!

They were made of ... well, perhaps I won't tell you. But you can probably guess ...